# EGMONT
*We bring stories to life*

First published in Great Britain 2009
by Egmont UK Limited,
239 Kensington High Street, London W8 6SA

Postman Pat® © 2009 Woodland Animations Ltd, a division of Entertainment Rights PLC.
Licensed by Entertainment Rights PLC.
Original writer John Cunliffe. Royal Mail and Post Office imagery is used by kind
permission of Royal Mail Group plc. All rights reserved.

ISBN 978 1 4052 4580 7

1 3 5 7 9 10 8 6 4 2

Printed in Germany

FSC
Mixed Sources
Product group from well-managed
forests and other controlled sources
Cert no. TT-COC-002332
www.fsc.org
© 1996 Forest Stewardship Council

Egmont is passionate about helping to preserve the world's remaining ancient forests.
We only use paper from legal and sustainable forest sources.

This book is made from paper certified by the Forestry Stewardship Council (FSC),
an organisation dedicated to promoting responsible management of forest resources.
For more information on the FSC, please visit www.fsc.org. To learn more about
Egmont's sustainable paper policy, please visit www.egmont.co.uk/ethical

# Postman Pat's Precious Special Delivery

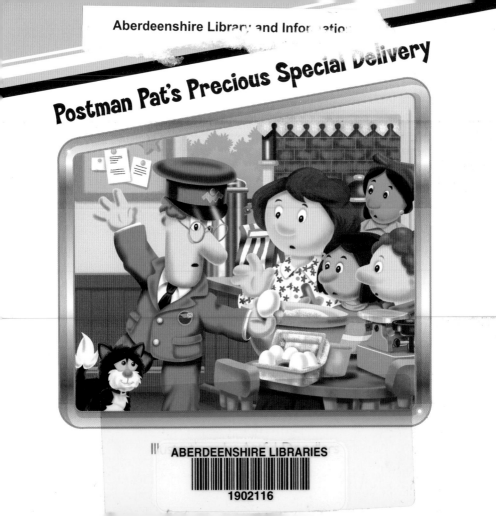

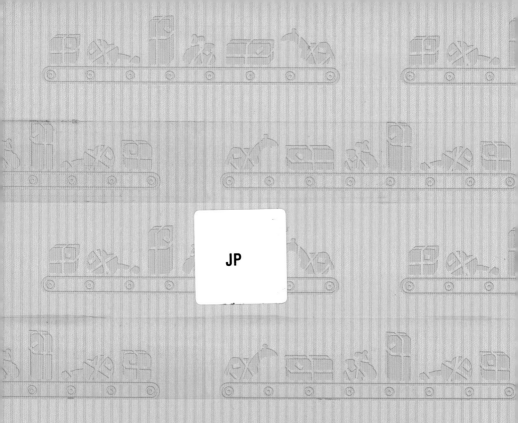

**JP**

Postman Pat will have to be extra-specially careful when he is asked to deliver a box of eggs to Amy. And these are no ordinary eggs! It's a race against time to save the Greendale ducklings!

Postman Pat and Jess were having a quiet day. Suddenly, Postman Pat's phone rang its special ring.

"Special Delivery Service, Postman Pat speaking," he answered.

It was Ben, at the mail centre, calling to tell Postman Pat there was a package for immediate delivery.

Postman Pat jumped into the van with Jess.

When Postman Pat got to Pencaster, it was market day and PC Selby had closed the road.

"You'll have to park here and walk, Pat," he called.

But Postman Pat didn't have time for that. He borrowed a bicycle and jumped onto it. He whizzed off at high speed, with Jess in the basket.

At the mail centre, Ben showed Postman Pat the special delivery.

"These are duck eggs," Ben explained. "Greendale pond is going to have six baby ducklings. You must get them to Amy quickly. She will keep them warm until they hatch."

"That really is a special delivery," said Postman Pat. "We'd better get going!"

As Postman Pat was carrying the precious eggs back to his van, he met Mrs Goggins and Bonnie. Bonnie leapt up at Jess and chased him through the market. Jess hid under a stall.

Postman Pat put the eggs down on the stall while he crawled underneath to rescue Jess.

"Don't worry, Jess," he said kindly. "Bonnie is only playing."

But when Postman Pat stood up again, the eggs had disappeared!

"I'm afraid Michael just bought them for his mobile shop," explained Dorothy. "I didn't know they were special. They looked just like the others."

"Oh, dear," said Postman Pat. "Come on, Jess. We might catch him if we hurry!"

Postman Pat drove his van as fast as possible along the lane. But at the corner, he had to stop suddenly. Alf's sheep were blocking the road!

Jess jumped out of the van, and herded the sheep through the gate.

"I've heard of a sheepdog," laughed Alf, as Postman Pat and Jess drove off. "But a sheepcat . . . now I've seen it all!"

In the village, Sara was out doing some shopping.

"Hello, Michael," she said. "Nisha and I are making cakes. I need sugar, butter, flour and . . . eggs."

"No problem," said Michael giving her the ingredients. Sarah put the precious eggs in her basket and waved goodbye to Michael.

As Sara walked away she met Amy, who was looking worried.

"Amy, is everything alright?" she asked.

"You haven't seen Postman Pat have you?" replied Amy. "I'm waiting for a very special delivery."

"Don't worry," said Sara. "Pat won't let you down."

Postman Pat drove up to Michael's mobile shop in a hurry. He jumped out and rushed over.

"Have you got the eggs you bought from Dorothy?" asked Postman Pat, breathlessly.

"I'm sorry, Pat," replied Michael. "I've just sold them to Sara."

"I have to get over there right now," said Postman Pat, as he ran back to the van.

At the café, Sara, Nisha and the children were making cakes.

First they weighed the sugar. Then they mixed in the butter and the flour.

"Now for the eggs," said Sara.

She picked up an egg and was just about to crack it when . . .

"No-o-o-o-o-o-o-o!" shouted Postman Pat, bursting through the door. "Those aren't ordinary eggs! I have to get them to Amy so she can hatch them."

But at that moment, the eggs started to wobble and crack!

"We haven't got much time," said Postman Pat. "Jess can keep them warm until we get there."

"Have you got the eggs?" asked Amy, as Postman Pat drove up.

"I'm afraid not," he replied. "But I've got something better . . ."

Jess jumped out of the van followed by six baby ducks.

"They've hatched!" cried Amy. "And they think Jess is their mummy!"

"Special Delivery Service — mission accomplished!" laughed Postman Pat.

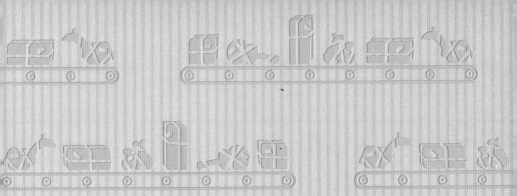

# My Postman Pat Story Library

## Start your Postman Pat® Story Library Collection NOW and look out for more titles to follow later!

Send off your Postman Pat token above for your free Postman Pat poster and door hanger to: POSTMAN PAT OFFERS, PO BOX 715, HORSHAM, RH12 5WG

To be completed by an adult

Please send me a Postman Pat poster and door hanger. I enclose a token as proof of purchase.

**Fan's name:**

**Address:**

**Postcode:**       **Date of birth:**

**Email:**

**Name of parent / guardian:**

**Signature of parent / guardian:**

Please allow 28 days for delivery. Offer only available while stocks last. We reserve the right to change the terms of this offer at any time. Offers apply to UK only. We may occasionally like to send you information about other Egmont children's books, including the next titles in the Postman Pat ® Story Library series. If you would rather we didn't please tick this box. ☐

Ref: PAT 001